E HAU
Hautzig, Deborah.
Little Witch's big night /
31112016632206

05062010

WITHDRAWN

Dear Parent:

Congratulations! Your child is taking
the first steps on an exciting journey.
The destination? Independent reading!

STEP INTO READING® will help your child get there. The program offers
books at five levels that accompany children from their first attempts at
reading to reading success. Each step includes fun stories, fiction and
nonfiction, and colorful art. There are also Step into Reading Sticker Books,
Step into Reading Math Readers, and Step into Reading Phonics Readers—
a complete literacy program with something to interest every child.

Learning to Read, Step by Step!

Ready to Read   Preschool–Kindergarten
• big type and easy words • rhyme and rhythm • picture clues
For children who know the alphabet and are eager to
begin reading.

Reading with Help   Preschool–Grade 1
• basic vocabulary • short sentences • simple stories
For children who recognize familiar words and sound out
new words with help.

Reading on Your Own   Grades 1–3
• engaging characters • easy-to-follow plots • popular topics
For children who are ready to read on their own.

Reading Paragraphs   Grades 2–3
• challenging vocabulary • short paragraphs • exciting stories
For newly independent readers who read simple sentences
with confidence.

Ready for Chapters   Grades 2–4
• chapters • longer paragraphs • full-color art
For children who want to take the plunge into chapter books
but still like colorful pictures.

STEP INTO READING® is designed to give every child a successful
reading experience. The grade levels are only guides. Children can progress
through the steps at their own speed, developing confidence in their
reading, no matter what their grade.

Remember, a lifetime love of reading starts with a single step!

Text copyright © 1984 by Random House, Inc. Illustrations copyright © 1984 by Marc Brown. All rights reserved under International and Pan-American Copyright Conventions. Published in the United States by Random House Children's Books, a division of Random House, Inc., New York, and simultaneously in Canada by Random House of Canada Limited, Toronto.

www.stepintoreading.com

Educators and librarians, for a variety of teaching tools, visit us at www.randomhouse.com/teachers

Library of Congress Cataloging-in-Publication Data
Hautzig, Deborah.
Little Witch's big night / by Deborah Hautzig ; illustrated by Marc Brown.
    p.   cm. — (Step into reading. A step 3 book)
SUMMARY: Little Witch, as punishment for cleaning up her room, has to stay home on Halloween night, but manages to have a good time anyway.
ISBN 0-394-86587-1 (trade) — ISBN 0-394-96587-6 (lib. bdg.)
[1. Witches—Fiction.   2. Halloween—Fiction.]
I. Brown, Marc Tolon, ill.   II. Title.   III. Series: Step into reading. Step 3 book.
PZ7.H2888   Lik   2003   [E]—dc21   2002013340

Printed in the United States of America   45 44 43 42 41 40 39

STEP INTO READING, RANDOM HOUSE, and the Random House colophon are registered trademarks of Random House, Inc.

STEP INTO READING®

STEP 3

Little Witch's Big Night

by Deborah Hautzig

illustrated by Marc Brown

Random House 🏠 New York

It was Halloween night.

All the witches were busy.

They were busy getting ready

for their Halloween ride.

Grouchy Witch was busy

making grouchy faces

in her cracked mirror.

Nasty Witch was busy
shooting a water gun
at her cat, Bow-Wow.

Mother Witch was busy
making a new broomstick
for Little Witch.

Oh, what a wonderful Halloween
it was going to be!

All the witches were ready . . .
but where was Little Witch?
"Little Witch, what are you doing?"
called Mother Witch.

Mother Witch went upstairs
and into Little Witch's room.
"What! You made your bed again!"
screeched Mother Witch.
"Sorry, Mother. I forgot,"
said Little Witch.

Then Mother Witch looked

under the bed.

"And you cleaned your cobwebs!"

Mother Witch was angry.

"You really must be punished.
You will stay home tonight
while we go flying,"
said Mother Witch.
"But it is Halloween!"
said Little Witch.

"Maybe this will teach you
not to be so good,"
said Mother Witch.

Little Witch watched
the big witches fly off.
Oh, how she wanted
to fly with them!
She was very sad.

Her bat, Scrubby,

wanted to cheer her up.

He made funny faces ...

and he did silly tricks.

"Even my bat is good!"

cried Little Witch.

"This is the worst Halloween ever."

Suddenly—

ding, dong went the doorbell.

Little Witch ran to the door.

She opened it and saw

a devil,

a pirate,

and an astronaut.

Each had a big bag of candy.

"Trick or treat!"

they said.

"Oh, dear," said Little Witch.

"I have no treats for you."

"No treats!" said the devil.

"No treats!" said the pirate.

"No treats!" said the astronaut.

"But it is Halloween!"

said the three trick-or-treaters.

They started to walk away.

"Wait," said Little Witch.

"Maybe I can

give you a treat."

"I can give you a ride
on my broomstick,"
she said.

"Really?" said the devil.

"Wow!" said the pirate.

"Can you really fly?"
asked the astronaut.

"Just wait and see!"
said Little Witch proudly.

"But there is room for just two
on my broomstick."
The devil said, "Me first!"

Little Witch sat in front.

She said some magic words:

"Horrible borrible,

Spinach pie,

Come on, broomstick,

Fly, fly, fly!"

WHOOSH! The broomstick

shot off the porch

and up into the sky.

Up and up they flew.
The houses and trees looked
like little toys.
Little Witch said
more magic words:

"Bibbety boppety,
Lizard soup,
Broomstick, do a
Loop-the-loop!"

The broomstick did

a perfect loop-the-loop.

"Wow!" said the devil.

"You really are

a wonderful witch."

"Thank you,"

said Little Witch.

"And now . . .

"Alakazoo,

Four-leaf clover,

Back we fly—

Your turn is over."

THUMP! The broomstick landed
back on the porch.
Next it was the pirate's turn.
"Hold on tight!"
said Little Witch.
And with another big WHOOSH
they zoomed into the sky.

Soon they were flying
over the ocean.
Below them was
a real pirate ship!

The pirate captain looked up.
He did not believe
what he saw.
"Shiver me timbers!
A witch and a flying pirate!"
he shouted.
Little Witch and her friend
waved to the pirate captain.

"Now we will fly home—
backward!"
said Little Witch.
She said the magic words:

"Mumbo jumbo,
Broomy stick,
Take us home—
And make it quick!"

They zoomed backward,
over the ocean,
over the town,
and back to Little Witch's porch.

"Now it is my turn!"
said the astronaut.
She got onto the broomstick
and Little Witch said:

"Hocus-pocus,

Peanut stew,

Here's a broomstick

Ride for you!"

And—WHOOSH—they were off.

Little Witch and the astronaut
flew over the big city.
They whizzed around
the tall buildings.

They saw jack-o'-lanterns
in the windows.
The jack-o'-lanterns winked
at them.
Little Witch and the astronaut
winked right back.

"Can you fly upside down?"
asked the astronaut.
"Yes, I can!"
said Little Witch,
and she said the magic words:

"Harum-scarum,
Witches' vats,
Now we're hanging
Just like bats!"

Flip-flop!

Upside down they flew

over the roofs and past the moon.

Then the broomstick took them back
to Little Witch's porch.
The three trick-or-treaters
clapped their hands.
"This was the best Halloween yet!"
they said.
"Let's go flying next year too!"
Little Witch smiled.
"That's a good idea,"
she said.
"Well, good-bye," said the devil,
the pirate, and the astronaut.
"And thank you!"

Little Witch waved good-bye
to her friends.

Then she swept the porch.

"I will be very good all year,"

she told Scrubby.

"Then Mother will punish me

and I can fly again

with my new friends."

Little Witch was reading
a bedtime story to Scrubby
when the big witches came home.

Grouchy Witch said,
"You missed the spookiest
Halloween ever!"

Nasty Witch said,
"We scared all the children!"

Mother Witch said,
"I hope you learned
your lesson."

"Because," said Mother Witch,
"I learned MY lesson.
Halloween is not fun
without you.
I missed you, Little Witch!"

Then she gave Little Witch
a big Halloween hug.

At bedtime Mother Witch told
Little Witch a spooky story.

Then she tucked her in.
"Next year you can fly
with us. I promise,"
said Mother Witch.
"Can I bring some friends?"
asked Little Witch.
"Yes—if you promise
not to be too good,"
said Mother Witch.

"I will do my best, Mother,"
said Little Witch.
And she really meant it.
Then Little Witch fell asleep
and dreamed about
the best Halloween ever.